Night and Day

a Night Stalkers CSAR romance story
by
M. L. Buchman

Buchman Bookworks

Other works by M.L. Buchman

<u>The Night Stalkers</u>

MAIN FLIGHT

The Night Is Mine
I Own the Dawn
Wait Until Dark
Take Over at Midnight
Light Up the Night
Bring On the Dusk
By Break of Day

WHITE HOUSE HOLIDAY

Daniel's Christmas
Frank's Independence Day
Peter's Christmas
Zachary's Christmas
Roy's Independence Day

AND THE NAVY

Christmas at Steel Beach
Christmas at Peleliu Cove

5E

Target of the Heart
Target Lock on Love

<u>Firehawks</u>

MAIN FLIGHT

Pure Heat
Full Blaze
Hot Point
Flash of Fire

SMOKEJUMPERS

Wildfire at Dawn
Wildfire at Larch Creek
Wildfire on the Skagit

Delta Force
Target Engaged
Heart Strike

Angelo's Hearth
Where Dreams are Born
Where Dreams Reside
Maria's Christmas Table
Where Dreams Unfold
Where Dreams Are Written

Eagle Cove
Return to Eagle Cove
Recipe for Eagle Cove
Longing for Eagle Cove
Keepsake for Eagle Cove

Deities Anonymous
Cookbook from Hell: Reheated
Saviors 101

Dead Chef Thrillers
Swap Out!
One Chef!
Two Chef!

SF/F Titles
Nara
Monk's Maze
Newsletter signup at: www.mlbuchman.com

1

Flying had always been a joy. This was less like flying and more like floating. Lieutenant Nicolai Martin tried to pin down the difference, but couldn't quite put his finger on it. That itself should say something about him…he knew it should…he could remember it from training…but he couldn't quite bring it into focus.

He shrugged it off.

And the blast of pain that lanced up his left shoulder snapped him out of it.

"*Derr'mo!*" Oh. He remembered the training now.

"In English, Nicolai." Vasily couldn't even curse in Russian which was why Nicolai always made a point of doing so around him. Though his French could be vitriolic, even if you could hear the Secaucus, New Jersey loud and clear behind it.

"Shit!" Nicolai repeated as he struggled to catch his breath through the blinding pain. Now he could easily picture the page in the manual: *Typical shock reactions to being shot.*

"No kidding!"

Nicolai blinked hard, forcing his eyes to focus. It was pitch dark except for the soft glow of the instruments on the console—the console of their MH-47G Chinook helicopter. They were the Night Stalkers of the 160th Special Operations Aviation Regiment, and SOAR ruled the night. The Chinook was a massive twin-rotor, heavy-lifter, the monster of SOAR's fleet.

Captain Vasily Carlsen sat to his right, his hands on the flight controls. Between the two of them, their helicopter had become known as "The Russian Bird" even though they were just a couple of good-looking second-generation Slavs from New Jersey. His and

Vasily's facility with the ladies had only added to the reputation. Vasily couldn't speak a word of Russian, but he wasn't above affecting the accent. Unlike Nicolai's, it was a really shitty accent, but still it worked on the ladies.

Nicolai closed his eyes again for a moment, looking for that pleasant floating feeling of a few moments ago…and not really finding it. Hard to do in the middle of a firefight. The three crew chiefs in the back were from strange places like Colorado and Arkansas. They were busy hammering away at the enemy with their guns.

Tonight they had post-mission dates lined up with a couple of hot lieutenants fresh in from stateside—curvy California blondes, his favorite kind of lieutenant. As a bonus pack, they were both Air Force, which cured most of the fraternization issues. For some reason the California girls in particular ate up the Russian accent. Even imagining that didn't get him back to the floating place that had been so nice a moment ago.

Nicolai opened his eyes again. Careful to use his right hand, he flipped his main screen onto the HUMS display. The Chinook's health and usage monitoring system was reporting complete and utter mayhem.

Double *Derr'mo!* "The Russian Bird" was not very healthy at the moment. Careful again to use his right hand, he flipped down his Night-Vision Goggles. Right. That's when he'd been shot. The FLIR had been shot out, he'd reached up with his left hand to shove the dead visor feed aside and pull down his NVGs. Being shot in his raised left arm was probably all that had saved him from being shot in the face.

They'd made their delivery: two men in a battered Toyota Corolla, one of the most common cars in Pakistan, delivered at the dead of night on a deserted road outside of Islamabad. No questions were asked and no explanations were offered. Some missions were like that, usually ones for the CIA or other intelligence guys simply known as The Activity. Total time "The Russian Bird" was on the ground after a two-hour flight? Twenty-three seconds. Then they and their escort Black Hawk had turned for home, Bagram Airfield, Afghanistan.

The four hundred kilometer flight should

have been a quiet passage as they were moving low and fast, and well off the more fortified paths.

When they hit the Safēd Kōh mountains, carefully well north of the hazardous Khyber Pass and deep into no man's land, they should have been clear. Except for that random patrol by a PAF fighter. The Pakistani Armed Forces tended to shoot first and ask questions later. The dogfight had been brief and ugly, thankfully the Paki pilot hadn't thought to go to missiles before Ed in the Black Hawk had. They'd managed to down the aged F-16A, but not before he did some damage…and called in for help.

Even though the Pakis and the US were technically allies, tonight's mission wasn't exactly something the US could admit to or ask permission for. Additional PAF forces had harassed Nicolai's and Vasily's helicopter well into Afghan airspace—high in the mountains, borders were a matter of great debate and little attention.

With the NVGs down, he could see that there was nothing outside to see unless he was doing the flying, which was Vasily's problem at the moment.

The Pakistanis had finally fallen behind as their own flight had descended into the western range. Running the Chinook low and dark was all that saved them.

However, the air battle attracted the attention of the Taliban ground forces who had taken over the game, peppering them with small fire as they passed too close to Asadabad. Some of it not so small.

"At least no one had time to grab an RPG," he managed. If they had, the Chinook would be a thousand little pieces raining down over the glaciers.

Vasily grunted, too busy to do more.

Nicolai knew he should be helping him, but he was having trouble thinking what to do. The adrenal surge wasn't going to hold off the real pain and panic for much longer. He forced himself to hold focus against the desire to drift away from this mess.

A Chinook was a massive and tough bird with big twin rotors, bigger engines, and the power to carry forty troops or lift a howitzer. Its only defense was a pair of mini-guns, one to either side and a ramp gun at the rear, all in the hands of the crew chiefs.

The three weapons were currently at full roar, meaning he was the only one available to try and save the helicopter.

The M60 ramp gun was hammering away and the two miniguns were barking their buzz-saw *Brap!*, spitting thousands of rounds a minute in short lethal bursts. The noise was so loud that even the flight helmet offered little defense against it. Still, he'd rather be on this end than the receiving end.

They still had two engines, but the oil pressure was sliding on one of them.

On the tracking radar, he found Ed's Black Hawk, their heavy weapons escort…but they had taken the brunt of the PAF and Tali attack. They weren't firing a thing.

"Vasily, I got nothing here. Heading back to base." Ed called over the radio.

"Roger," Vasily acknowledged because there wasn't anything else to say. The Hawk wouldn't abandon them unless he truly had "nothing." It meant that he had so much systems damage, he couldn't even fire. Hopefully that damage wasn't to his human systems, but that might explain his choice to race across the last hundred kilometers back to base.

They were on their own. The main problem—slashed across the status reading on the HUMS—was that there were limits to what the aircraft could take. And they were reaching it.

They certainly couldn't climb enough to clear the final ridge between them and the dry plains leading to Bagram Air Base. Or even much more level flying.

Very gingerly Nicolai raised his left arm.

Big mistake!

That's when it finally slammed into his brain what was wrong in more than a merely academic way.

His hiss of pain must have alerted Vasily. Or perhaps that he wasn't doing much to help with checking all the systems that were presently begging for attention.

"What?" Vasily snapped out.

"I just wish the Chinook was the only 'Russian' that had been shot tonight."

2

Gerta Kozlov sat at the table in the pilot's ready room at Bagram Air Base practicing her hurry-up-and-wait with a game of solitaire. Two pilots and a pair of crew chiefs were watching television. By their easy chatter, it was clear they had been together for a long time…this was her very first watch as a medic. Despite the thirty hours in transit from the states, her nerves hadn't let her sleep and she was still wide awake. Maybe with the dawn she'd be able to sleep.

In the early evening before the first briefing, she had gone for a run around the base, racking up a quick 5K just to keep herself loose. Bagram Air Base was one of the oddities of America's partial return to Afghanistan. For years it had been among the world's largest and busiest air bases with forty thousand people and a hundred and forty thousand flights a year—averaging once every four minutes around the clock. Now, the perimeter defenses had been pulled in until the base was one-third its former size, and still it was an echoing void inside the fortifications. Long lines of abandoned platforms showed where massive bunkroom tents had once stood. Whole hangers were filled with the burned and battered remains of a fleet of trucks, destroyed past use during the war. No longer in good enough shape to take home nor worth destroying further to keep them out of unfriendly hands—the piles of blackened and twisted metal were of no use to anyone.

She lay a red queen on the king of clubs. This was the war she had come to.

She had defected from the Russian Ukraine three years ago, a weapons officer of rank, rescued by Sergeant Connie Davis during a Night Stalkers black op. To pay back the kindness, she had made her way into the Night Stalkers as a medic. And, even though the US was only here in an "advisory" role, as usual the 160th SOAR's helicopters were here to do far more than advise.

The next card up was the suicide king. *Perfect!* She had nowhere for him to go.

There were several missions on tonight, though of course no one had said what they were. Their own aircraft had scouted an Al-Qaeda cell, but left it to the drone pilots to take care of once they'd confirmed the location. They'd returned to base hours ago, but remained at Alert Status in the ready room in case something went wrong with one of the other missions still out. With so few resources on the ground in Afghanistan, they were stretched very thin.

Go!

Cards scattered as she jolted to her feet. Her medical backpack was half on before the sound of the alarm fully registered. The pilot and crew were just as fast to their feet.

Gerta liked that. In the Ukrainian military, first there would be curses, then complaining. After that a pilot was as likely as not to knock back the rest of his vodka before even considering to get his sorry ass moving. The Special Operations Forces of the US military were like Red Fury, *the* kickass heroine of Russian comic books. Gerta had considered dying her short blond hair red just for the effect, but she didn't have the comic book chest—or much of a chest at all really—so it couldn't work.

Her mother was the one who had the figure that would never stop. She'd used it to crawl into a general's bed and who knew how many others. Her father didn't mind, it gave him more time with his mistress.

Gerta had taken after her father's lean form, his military calling, and as little else as she could manage.

"Let's move, comrade." They called out, even though she was already in the middle of the pack. Explaining that "comrade" was an outdated Communist term now more of an insult than anything had only anchored the nickname. No matter how hard she tried, she couldn't shake her thick Russian accent.

"Chinook going down with injuries," the watch commander said as he handed off a sheet of coordinates. "I'll send a repair crew as soon as I get one. Go secure that site!"

And they went.

Climbing aboard the heavily armed Black Hawk was so reminiscent of the moment that had changed her life three years before. This airfield was in the Afghan desert instead of the lush farm country of the central Ukraine, so the smells were wrong. But the night, the noise of the helicopter winding to life, the kerosene of Jet A fuel on the air, her gut clenching in fear…these were all familiar.

On that long ago night, a Night Stalkers team on a black op had landed deep inside foreign territory, her territory. The first she'd known of it had been when a Delta Force operator had whispered from mere feet away that if she so much as flinched, she'd die. Gerta had been very careful not to flinch. She had pleaded her way aboard their helicopter: unwanted, untrusted, but needed for the knowledge she alone possessed. Gerta had managed to prove herself and barter that knowledge for freedom.

Now, she was once again the unknown factor to an American Black Hawk crew. Of course that would be how it was even if she wasn't Ukrainian—the first day joining an already intact crew. The mistrust was there, though at least this time it didn't include wrist cuffs and a weapon hard against her chin. Her wrists ached with the memory.

This wasn't a dedicated medevac bird, so its cargo bay wasn't pre-hung with medical supplies and heart monitors. All she had was the forty-pound pack she was wearing. However, as she was just a medic along for a ride, rather than riding in an aerial ambulance, they weren't required to have the red cross on the outside nor did they have to leave their weapons behind. She liked being safe inside a helicopter with all its defenses in place.

They covered the hundred kilometers in under twenty minutes.

3

Nicolai did what he could to help. Engine Two flamed out shortly after hydraulic systems One and Two went south, probably dumping oil into the engine itself. The former problem was solved by pulling the engine's emergency T-handle cutting fuel and flooding the space with an extinguisher. The latter was simply a matter of praying that the backup hydraulic system was still intact. It was. He made sure that the One and Two systems shut down automatically. Two needed some help, but he got it.

There was an odd whistle, he could hear

it only in the gaps between the on-going gun battle. But it was loud enough to hear through his helmet.

"Change collective pitch for a second, Vasily. But don't do it too fast." With his left arm out of commission, he couldn't work the control which was beside his seat.

When Vasily did, the tone of the whistle changed. "A lot of holes in the rotor blades." And one in him. Shit! Even thinking about it made it hurt more.

"Perfect!"

"You mean *ideal'no!*" Nicolai grunted it out to distract himself from the pain. Satellite radio was out as was any hint of broadband.

Vasily groaned along with their dying helicopter. He'd steadfastly refused to learn even a single word of Russian. His grandparents had made such a big deal out of it that he'd studied French instead.

"Or *chudesnyy* if you want 'wonderful.'" He could feel the wetness all down his left sleeve, but needed his hand free to help save all their lives. For now he let the blood flow and just hoped it wasn't too much.

"I want to not die, in English or Russian,"

Vasily growled as he managed to nurse the Chinook over a ridge with less than five meters to spare above the ice field.

"How about in Chinese?" Descending over the other side of the ridge cut off the last of the Taliban gunfire. If there were Talis here, his team was going to be even more dead than they already were.

"Do you speak Chinese?"

"Nope."

"Then shut up."

"Can't help myself. Gallows humor." Nicolai gave up trying to restart the FLIR.

The Forward Looking Infrared cameras themselves must be gone. The NVGs weren't nearly as good, but even though the night was moonless, it wasn't starless, which gave him enough to see by.

"Plus, I'm charming. Just wait until we catch up with those blondes tonight." He began searching for signs of an opening big enough to land in, and any heat signatures of enemy lying in wait.

"C'mon, Nicolai. Find me something," Vasily's tense voice came from far away.

"*Nado zhe!*"

" 'Wow!' what?"

"See? I knew you understood Russian." Nicolai blinked hard to keep his eyes focused. "*Nado zhe,* but I feel a real need to learn how to pray, fast."

Then he saw it.

"Stream bed. Might be a sandbar. Five hundred yards out. Come right ten degrees and you'll see it.

Somehow Vasily got them down in one piece.

It wasn't pretty, landing shock jarred his arm badly.

He remembered starting to scream, but he wasn't conscious to hear when he stopped.

4

"This, it is longer than twenty minutes," Gerta finally complained over the intercom.

"Damned ridge and valley. Doesn't let a signal travel ten lousy clicks," either the pilot or copilot complained. She barely knew their names, and all Americans sounded alike to her. Especially the military ones. They seemed to take pleasure in removing all of the joy and expression from a language and turning it into a clipped monotone—as if English wasn't such a flat language in the first place.

"Got them," another voice declared. "How did they fit that big bird into that little spot?"

She slid open the side door and a blast of chill Afghan mountain air blew into the cargo bay. She leaned out and, flipping down the NVGs attached to her helmet, she looked around. The big Chinook was perched on a sandbar in the middle of a rough river. A boulder field spread up either steep bank, beginning just meters from the tips of its slowly spinning rotors. It appeared to be the only safe landing in the whole valley.

"Unfriendlies coming up over the ridge," someone called.

When her helicopter began to climb back away from the Chinook, Gerta called out.

"*Nyet!* I must be down there. Man is hurt."

"Nowhere to land."

She kicked out a Fast Rope. The one and three-quarter inch twisted rope spilled down forty meters, nowhere near the ground. "You will get me back down there now!" Gerta reached out and grabbed the rope in her thickly gloved hands. She dumped the monkey line that was the only thing attaching her to the helicopter.

"She's on the rope," one of the crew chiefs called.

"Shit!" The pilot could yell at her when they got back to base. He dropped elevation quickly even as she slid down the rope. She hit the water three meters after she ran out of rope. It was knee deep and bitterly cold, but it cushioned her fall a little from the hard sand below. The rope slithered down beside her as they released it from the helicopter, splashing in and then sweeping away like a water snake in the rushing current.

Gerta slogged up onto the sandbar. There was barely room to walk between the helicopter and the river. She knocked on the pilot's door.

His window slid open and the business end of a FN-SCAR rifle popped out close to her face.

She almost gave her Ukrainian rank, "Starshyi Leitenant Gerta Kozlov." Her American rank, Specialist, with her name would also sound very Russian. She decided that her life expectancy would be better if she simply said, "Medic."

"Oh. Other side."

She had to circle around the nose of the helicopter, wading back into the icy water. She saw that the FLIR camera which hung under the Chinook's nose was shattered. Through her NVGs she started noticing the numerous small circles in the metal skin where the starlight was *not* reflected back. Bullet holes. A great number of them.

The copilot's door, that she had to stand in a foot of water to reach, had a half dozen holes drilled into it.

"Not good. Very not good," she imagined herself saying in a slow, heavy tone; the way Americans thought all Russians spoke. At least in Hollywood films.

She knocked again, not wanting to face the front of another combat assault rifle. When there was no answer, she unlatched and opened the door. By the slant of his head, the copilot was out cold and would be little threat to her.

Gerta peeled off her heavy combat gloves that had protected her hands down the Fast Rope. Underneath them she wore doubled nitrile gloves that she'd put on during the flight.

A quick check at his neck…pulse strong and steady. But she could see the high heat of his blood on his flight suit; it stood out brilliant green in her NVGs as it was the hottest thing on the cold night.

"I need him out of seat," she called out as she undid his harness.

"So pull him out," the pilot called busy with other matters.

"If I do this, I am dumping him in river."

Suddenly the pilot leaned over and looked at her, with his rifle turned around to face her once again. "What's a Russian doing in US Army togs?"

"What is togs? Your copilot he is hurt. And I am not Russian! I am not even Ukrainian any more." Though not yet American. She needed two more years as a resident before she could apply for citizenship. *You can fight for us, but you can not vote.* As if voting ever made a difference in any government. "You want him alive or dead?"

"Shit!" The pilot cursed before shouting toward the back of the helo. "Nick. Alfie. Marco. Get this shot-up asshole out of my cockpit and dump him on a stretcher for the medic."

In a moment, the body was gone from between them, dragged backward through the narrow passageway to the rear. The pilot leaned closer now that the injured pilot was out of the way.

"You better be a damn good medic, sister. If a man as good as him dies at your hands, I'm going to be a very unhappy soldier."

She didn't even bother answering, it wasn't worth her time. Her father had grown to be a great Ukrainian general, until he'd betrayed their country and helped give Crimea to the Russians. An American captain knew nothing about how to deliver a threat.

Gerta sloshed back to the rear cargo ramp, stalked past the ramp gunner who was still on his feet so not her concern, and crossed the long cargo bay. Whatever their mission had been, it hadn't been to pick someone up. The cargo bay was empty except for the other two crew chiefs—smeared in dark hydraulic fluid or oil from a line they were working on, hydraulic by the sharp smell—and her patient.

There was a rattle of several shots hitting nearby stones, and one bright thunk as a single round hit metal. There was an answering hail of fire from the Black Hawk circling somewhere far above.

She knelt and got to work.

5

Nicolai came to flat on his back with a woman bent low over him. It was about what he'd been hoping for this evening…though not quite who he'd been hoping for.

Yes, the woman scowling down at him had blond hair, but it was nearly a crewcut. It did nothing to soften the lean lines of her narrow face; instead it made her look tough and scrappy.

Was she long and lean all the way? A quick glance further down the way revealed that her US Army flightsuit wasn't going to reveal anything further down the way. That forced his attention back to her face…and about the damn bluest eyes he'd ever seen.

"*Khorosho!*" The medic's voice was deep and fluid, like that floating place he'd been lost in. "You have decided that you are going to be living. Very good."

"*Da!* It is far better than being among the deading." That earned him a bit of a laugh. "Being dead would just ruin my whole day." More laughter.

"It's now night," she said as she shone a bright light into his eyes with that flick thing doctors did to be irritating.

"Night and day, day and night. Me and you, you and me." He sang it to a Marianas Trench song on his playlist. "Maybe we should become songwriters together."

His eyes were focusing better—now that she had the bright light out of them—and though he could hear the laughter, he could see that it wasn't coming from the spare blonde bending over him. It was…

He closed his mouth and the laugh stopped.

Great job, Nicolai. Making a fool of yourself in front of the woman.

Then she did something to his arm and he didn't feel like laughing at all.

"*B'lyad!* Stop that, you *cuchka derganaya!*"

"Can you do nothing beside cursing in bad Russian? And yes, I am a crazy bitch so do not make a mess with me."

Maybe he shouldn't have said that. Since there were no Californians around, he'd make the best of the situation. "It's just 'Don't mess with me.' And *da!* I can do more. I can make *sumasshedshiy* love in Russian."

"Crazy love. Just what a woman is to want." She continued working on his arm.

He started to raise his head to look.

She stopped him with the back of a gloved hand laid gently against his cheek. He could feel the heat of her through her thin gloves.

Once again those blue eyes took all of his attention.

"How are you with the sight of blood?"

"Fine," he reconsidered. "As long as it isn't mine."

"Then don't look," she nudged him back into his prone position.

As he lay there watching her eyes, he began focusing more easily. A bag of clear fluid hung above him, with a long tube descending toward his other arm. Despite the drugs she must have pumped into him, he wasn't feeling the least bit floaty. Nick and Alfie rushed by. At first he thought they were bloody too, then recognized the dark red of hydraulic fluid.

He should be helping them, except—

Shot! He now remembered that.

"How bad?"

"*Nichego.* Nothing," she shrugged as if it was even less than nothing. "If you were strong Ukrainian man rather than American wimp, you would be making mad love to me right now instead of lying there."

"It's a deal!" He tried to sit up as a tease, but agreeing to make love to her didn't get him very far before flopping back. "Maybe a rain check."

"What is rain check?"

After he explained she actually smiled. Damn but she had a smile. It turned lean, tough, and scrappy into striking.

He spent the rest of her repair of his arm, and the crew's repair of the helicopter trying to get her to laugh. And while he didn't quite succeed, her smile was a plenty nice reward for his efforts. He barely noticed when another two mechanics came up the rear ramp with a load of parts. The outside gun battle had never climbed past sporadic. They must be Night Stalker mechanics because they soon had the Chinook limping back up into the sky.

It left the two of them in a cocoon that worked all the way back to base.

He was fine by the time they landed at Bagram, other than being weak as a fish from blood loss. He'd been leaking out of three holes, but the bullets had been slowed down by the Chinook's armor enough that they hadn't done any major damage.

"Better my arm than my pretty face," he grimaced at how close a call that had been. "How long before I can fly again?"

"My guess," the medic ventured. "If in Ukraine, two weeks and you return to your flight duty. In America, four weeks."

"Great! How about taking that rain check with me? Somewhere quiet. A place with some palm trees."

"Some place like your tent," the sarcasm was thick in any language. If his own family was anything to go by, Slavs weren't subtle about what they were feeling. He loved them for it, and now it made the medic stand out from a thousand gentler, Americanized women. Her emotions were right on the surface and twice life-sized. It was like night and day, just as he'd said. The softer Californian girls, so bright in the daylight, and this overly serious Ukrainian who glowed in the night.

"Nah! Not my tent," he smiled up at her as she escorted his stretcher off the aircraft. "I have a CHU of my very own. Much better." His Containerized Housing Unit was still pretty lame: a bunk, a desk, a shower, and an air conditioner—but it was better than a tent. "Though I'd have to buy a palm tree, or draw a picture of one."

That finally earned him the laugh he was after. She gave herself to the laugh, her head back, the long lines of her face finally coming into form with the true smile. She laughed like a Russian, big and loud. She'd peeled down the upper half of her flightsuit and tied its arms around her waist. Lean, all the way down, and it looked absolutely amazing on her.

"I know! We can always get married in Italy. They have palm trees there somewhere."

"No," and still that glorious laugh bubbled beneath the surface. "I like you, but no."

"Why not?"

"Because," she stepped back as they carried him into an operating theater to finish the work she'd already done to save his life.

He twisted against the pain to look back at her.

"Because," she unleashed that smile once more. "I could never love a man with such a terrible Russian accent."

"*Derr'mo!* I'll have to work on that."

Her laugh got him through the short operation…well, until he saw the mass of bloody bandages they were peeling away from his arm.

6

Gerta was amazed at the operational tempo. In the Ukrainian Army, at least until the Russians invaded, there was very little to do. Even after they did, you were either on the line, or you weren't. She'd been responsible for a few carefully hidden weapons of mass destruction, so she'd never been near the line.

The Night Stalkers often flew several missions a night. Drop off Delta operators a kilometer from a suspected terrorist cell. Deliver a team of Rangers to help secure a forward operating base coming under heavy attack. Extract the Deltas and deliver them to their next strike point, before dropping a SEAL team into a river to float down into the center of a hostile town that wouldn't be nearly as hostile by the time they were done with it.

In two weeks, she had already lost count of the number of missions. She'd saved two more American lives, fifteen local Afghan forces, and patched half a hundred injuries barely worth reporting. A bar brawl involving a regular Army unit and an Explosive Ordnance Disposal squad had created the most casualties. The EODs were badly outnumbered, but those guys were tough. No one understood teamwork like a demolition squad, not even the Night Stalkers. The fact that Bagram was a dry base had landed all their asses in hack for illicit alcohol. Not her problem.

"Comrade" had now proved herself and was a welcome member of the team, though the nickname hadn't gone away. She was actually becoming attached to it.

Gerta was crawling back to her CHU with the dawn after a particularly busy night. At the door she had to tip her head back and forth several times before she could make sense of what had been taped to the door. Cut out of brown shipping paper and colored with magic marker stood…a foot high palm tree. It was placed as if it was growing from the dusty threshold.

She looked around, but didn't see Nicolai Martin anywhere.

Very carefully, she peeled off the tree, carried it inside, and taped it back up on exactly the same spot inside her door.

She had saved and helped many, but none other had made her laugh. Or even smile, except to herself—pleased to have saved another life. She'd earned a reputation during training of being a total hard-ass. It was an image that she hadn't minded at all. Being a general's daughter, she'd had very few friends— everyone was afraid of him. And she'd left the country very soon after he had betrayed it.

She'd only been at the base where the Night Stalkers had found her three years ago because of a horrible fight with her father, which turned out to be their final one. She'd driven back to work despite it being New Year's Eve—just in time for the Americans' raid.

"No one here. No one here," she had pleaded. "No family. Take me with you."

And they had. It was a lie she'd never regretted.

In honest truth, she did wish she hadn't been such a "hard-ass" since. There hadn't been anyone in America…but she couldn't stop smiling at the small, horribly-drawn palm tree.

For all of the next week, Gerta came back to her housing unit to palm trees. Tall ones that barely fit on her door. Small ones that grew up from the flange of the door knob. And one that showed only as leaves in the small window making it look as if it was growing inside.

By the end of the week, she had a palm forest taped to the inside of her door.

No notes.

No sudden appearances.

Just the trees.

7

They'd given him four weeks medical leave… and Nicolai had survived a week of it. He'd landed on an Italian beach, which was normally prime babe hunting ground. But every time he selected his target and made ready to chat up some likely tourist or Italian with honey-colored skin enveloping heavenly-shaped curves, he pictured those intense blue eyes and heard the medic's big Slavic laugh bursting from her lean frame.

He hit Aviano Air Base in Italy and hitched a ride back into the Afghanistan theater a couple of weeks ahead of any chance of the medicos releasing him to active flight duty. Still, it was an improvement. He'd been going stir-crazy sitting on his ass in Italy and just watching the scenery walk by—fine scenery though it was.

When he asked for something to keep him busy, classic Army thinking dropped him into a daytime job logging the night's duty rosters. It placed him in a whole different section of the base, so that he barely saw the rest of the crew. It also made him feel more like shit than ever that they were flying and he wasn't up there with them.

Wondering how the medic was doing was getting Nicolai all of nowhere.

Not even knowing her name, he couldn't track her down. At least not until he thought to look up his own record. Why it took him a week of slogging through the reports to think of that…

He was amused to note that all of his flirting had been reduced to a single sentence: "Upon regaining consciousness, patient displayed a positive attitude and a sense of humor."

Signed by Specialist Gerta Kozlov.

He didn't snoop in records or even ask

around, but he learned a lot about Gerta Kozlov anyway. Despite her recent arrival—he was her first-ever report—she was rapidly becoming the most active medic in the entire company. She always managed to be first on the scene, arrive with a full aid kit, and nothing but full marks from the follow-up medicos. He certainly didn't have any complaints—his problem wasn't his arm, it was boredom.

Merely hunting her down wasn't going to work.

Hi, I'm the guy who called you a "crazy bitch" during your first day on the job. And I'm sure you remember: while you were saving my life I offered to have sex with you. So, do you wanna do it?

Not smooth—not by his standard…not by any standard.

That's when he hit on the idea of the palm trees. He used his day schedule versus her night schedule to his advantage.

When she was aloft, he tracked down her CHU, his one bit of snooping, and made his palm trees. He didn't wait around to see if she liked them. He really didn't want to know if she didn't. Each morning they were gone while he was out on his run before going to work, and each night he tacked up a new one. Good thing none of the guys saw him or they'd know he'd lost it.

After a week though, he was running out of patience with himself. He needed to know what she was thinking…he really needed to know. Even it was bad news. Still, he couldn't think of a decent opening.

The morning after the medicos signed him off as healthy, he returned to his CHU. He'd slept okay that night—well, as okay as he ever did since Gerta Kozlov had invaded his thoughts—but he had to be mission-ready by nightfall. A Night Stalkers clock was flipped, always flying at night, and switching your schedule back and forth was a pain in the ass.

Even a daytime nap would help with the switchover, though he wasn't placing any bets.

He was half through the door to his CHU before he noticed anything.

In the corner of the window, taped to the glass, was a tiny palm tree. It was far more elegant than any that he had made.

Best of all, it was taped to the *inside* of the glass.

Through the partly open door, he could hear someone start singing.

"Night and day, day and night. Me and you, you and me," as if to herself.

And she was singing it in Russian.

He almost laughed aloud. Russian really was the language of wooing.

His accent might suck, but Gerta's sounded *wonderful*. He looked forward to listening to it for a long time to come.

About the Author

M. L. Buchman has over 50 novels and 30 short stories in print. His military romantic suspense books have been named Barnes & Noble and NPR "Top 5 of the year" and twice *Booklist* "Top 10 of the Year," placing two titles on their "Top 101 Romances of the Last 10 Years" list. He has been nominated for the Reviewer's Choice Award for "Top 10 Romantic Suspense of the Year" by *RT Book Reviews* and was a 2016 RWA RITA finalist. In addition to romance, he also writes thrillers, fantasy, and science fiction.

In among his career as a corporate project

manager he has: rebuilt and single-handed a fifty-foot sailboat, both flown and jumped out of airplanes, and designed and built two houses. Somewhere in there he also bicycled solo around the world.

He is now making his living as a full-time writer on the Oregon Coast with his beloved wife. He is constantly amazed at what you can do with a degree in Geophysics. You may keep up with his writing by subscribing to his newsletter at www.mlbuchman.com.

If you enjoyed this story, you might also enjoy:

Target of the Heart (excerpt)
-a Night Stalkers 5E novel-

Major Pete Napier hovered his MH-47G Chinook helicopter ten kilometers outside of Lhasa, Tibet and a mere two inches off the tundra. A mixed action team of Delta Force and The Activity—the slipperiest intel group on the planet—flung themselves aboard.

The additional load sent an infinitesimal shift in the cyclic control in his right hand. The hydraulics to close the rear loading ramp hummed through the entire frame of the massive helicopter. By the time his crew chief could reach forward to slap an "all secure" signal against his shoulder, they were already ten feet up and fifty out. That was enough altitude. He kept the nose down as he clawed for speed in the thin air at eleven thousand feet.

"Totally worth it," one of the D-boys announced as soon as he was on the Chinook's internal intercom.

He'd have to remember to tell that to the two Black Hawks flying guard for him…when they were in a friendly country and could risk a radio transmission. This deep inside China—or rather Chinese-held territory as the CIA's mission-briefing spook had insisted on calling it—radios attracted attention and were only used to avoid imminent death and destruction.

"Great, now I just need to get us out of this alive."

"Do that, Pete. We'd appreciate it."

He wished to hell he had a stealth bird like the one that had gone into bin Laden's compound. But the one that had crashed during that raid had been blown up. Where there was one, there were always two, but the second had gone back into hiding as thoroughly as if it had never existed. He hadn't heard a word about it since.

The Tibetan terrain was amazing, even if all he could see of it was the monochromatic green of night vision. And blackness. The largest city in Tibet lay a mere ten kilometers away and they were flying over barren wilderness. He could crash out here and no one would know for decades unless some yak herder stumbled upon them. Or were yaks in Mongolia? He was a corn-fed, white boy from Colorado, what did he know about Tibet? Most of the countries he'd flown into on black ops missions he'd only seen at night anyway.

While moving very, very fast.

Like now.

The inside of his visor was painted with overlapping readouts. A pre-defined terrain map, the best that modern satellite imaging could build made the first layer. This wasn't some crappy, on-line, look-at-a-picture-of-your-house display. Someone had a pile of dung outside their goat pen? He could see it, tell you how high it was, and probably say if they were pygmy goats or full-size LaManchas by the size of their shit-pellets if he zoomed in.

On top of that were projected the forward-looking infrared camera images. The FLIR imaging gave him a real-time overlay, in case someone had put an addition onto their goat shed since the last satellite pass, or parked their tractor across his intended flight path.

His nervous system was paying autonomic attention to that combined landscape. He also compensated for the thin air at altitude as he instinctively chose when to start his climb over said goat shed or his swerve around it.

It was the third layer, the tactical display that had most of his attention. At least he and the two Black Hawks flying escort on him were finally on the move.

To insert this deep into Tibet, without passing over Bhutan or Nepal, they'd had to add wingtanks on the Black Hawks' hardpoints where he'd much rather have a couple banks of

Hellfire missiles. Still, they had 20mm chain guns and the crew chiefs had miniguns which was some comfort.

While the action team was busy infiltrating the capital city and gathering intelligence on the particularly brutal Chinese assistant administrator, he and his crews had been squatting out in the wilderness under a camouflage net designed to make his helo look like just another god-forsaken Himalayan lump of granite.

Command had determined that it was better for the helos to wait on site through the day than risk flying out and back in. He and his crew had stood shifts on guard duty, but none of them had slept. They'd been flying together too long to have any new jokes, so they'd played a lot of cribbage. He'd long ago ruled no gambling on a mission, after a fistfight had broken out about a bluff hand that cost a Marine three hundred and forty-seven dollars. Marines hated losing to Army no matter how many times it happened. They'd had to sit on him for a long time before he calmed down.

Tonight's mission was part of an on-going campaign to discredit the Chinese "presence" in Tibet on the international stage—as if occupying the country the last sixty years didn't count toward ruling, whether invited or not. As usual, there was a crucial vote coming up at the U.N.—that, as usual, the Chinese could be guaranteed to ignore. However, the ever-hopeful CIA was in a hurry to make sure that any damaging information that they could validate was disseminated as thoroughly as possible prior to the vote.

Not his concern.

His concern was, were they going to pass over some Chinese sentry post at their top speed of a hundred and ninety-six miles an hour? The sentries would then call down a couple Shenyang J-16 jet fighters that could hustle along at Mach 2 to fry his sorry ass. He knew there was a pair of them parked at Lhasa along with some older gear that would be just as effective against his three helos.

"Don't suppose you could get a move on, Pete?"

"Eat shit, Nicolai!" He was a good man to have as a copilot. Pete knew he was holding on too tight, and Nicolai knew that a joke was the right way to ease the moment.

He, Nicolai, and the four pilots in the two Black Hawks had a long way to go tonight and he'd never make it if he stayed so tight on the controls that he could barely maneuver. Pete eased off and felt his fingers tingle with the rush of returning blood. They dove down into gorges and followed them as long as they dared. They hugged cliff walls at every opportunity to decrease their radar profile. And they climbed.

That was the true danger—they would be up near the helos' limits when they crossed over the backbone of the Himalayas in their rush for India. The air was so rarefied that they burned fuel at a prodigious rate. Their reserve didn't allow for any extended battles while crossing the border…not for any battle at all really.

# # #

It was pitch dark outside her helicopter when Captain Danielle Delacroix stamped on the left rudder pedal while giving the big Chinook right-directed control on the cyclic. It tipped her most of the way onto her side, but let her continue in a straight line. A Chinook's rotors were sixty feet across—front to back they overlapped to make the spread a hundred feet long. By cross-controlling her bird to tip it, she managed to execute a straight line between two mock pylons only thirty feet apart. They were made of thin cloth so they wouldn't down the helo if you sliced one—she was the only trainee to not have cut one yet.

At her current angle of attack, she took up less than a half-rotor of width, just twenty-four feet. That left her nearly three feet to either side, sufficient as she was moving at under a hundred knots.

The training instructor sitting beside her in the copilot's seat didn't react as she swooped through the training course at Fort Campbell, Kentucky. Only child of a single mother, she was used to providing her own feedback loops, so she didn't expect anything else. Those who expected outside validation rarely survived the SOAR induction testing, never mind the two years of training that followed.

As a loner kid, Danielle had learned that self-motivated congratulations and fun were much easier to come by than external ones. She'd spent innumerable hours deep in her mind as a pre-teen superheroine. At twenty-nine she was well on her way to becoming a real life one, though Helo-girl had never been a character she'd thought of in her youth.

External validation or not, after two years of training with the U.S. Army's 160th Special Operations Aviation Regiment she was ready for some action. At least *she* was convinced that she was. But the trainers of Fort Campbell, Kentucky had not signed off on anyone in her trainee class yet. Nor had they given any hint of when they might.

She ducked ten tons of racing Chinook under a bridge and bounced into a vertical climb to clear the power line on the far side. Like a ride on the toboggan at Terrassee Dufferin during *Le Carnaval de Québec,* only with five thousand horsepower at her fingertips. Using her Army signing bonus—the first money in her life that was truly hers—to attend *Le Carnaval* had been her one trip back to her birthplace since her mother took them to America when she was ten.

To even apply to SOAR required five years of prior military rotorcraft experience. She had applied after seven years because of a chance encounter—or rather what she'd thought was a chance encounter at the time.

Captain Justin Roberts had been a top Chinook pilot, the one who had convinced her to switch from her beloved Black Hawk and try out the massive twin-rotor craft. One flight and she'd been a goner, begging her commander until he gave in and let her cross over to the new platform. Justin had made the jump from the 10th Mountain Division to the 160th SOAR not long after that.

Then one night she'd been having pizza in Watertown, New York a couple miles off the 10th's base at Fort Drum.

"Danielle?" Justin had greeted her with the surprise of finding a good friend in an unexpected place. Danielle had liked Justin— even if he was a too-tall, too-handsome cowboy and completely knew it. But "good friend" was unusual for Danielle, with anyone, and Justin came close.

"Captain Roberts," as a dry greeting over the top edge of her Suzanne Brockmann novel didn't faze him in the slightest.

"Mind if I join ya?" A question he then answered for himself by sliding into the opposite seat and taking a slice of her pizza. She been thinking of taking the leftovers back to base, but that was now an idle thought.

"Are you enjoying life in SOAR?" she did her best to appear a normal, social human, a skill she'd learned by rote. *Greeting someone you knew after a time apart? Ask a question about them.* "They treating you well?"

"Whoo-ee, you have no idea, Danielle," his voice was smooth as…well, always…so she wouldn't think about it also sounding like a pickup line. He was beautiful, but didn't interest her; the outgoing ones never did.

"Tell me." *Men love to talk about themselves, so let them.*

And he did. But she'd soon forgotten about her novel, and would have forgotten the pizza if he hadn't reminded her to eat.

His stories shifted from intriguing to fascinating. There was a world out there that she'd been only peripherally aware of. The Night Stalkers of the 160th SOAR weren't simply better helicopter pilots, they were the most highly-trained and best-equipped ones on the planet. Their missions were pure razor's edge and black-op dark.

He'd left her with a hundred questions and enough interest to fill out an application to the 160th. Being a decent guy, Justin even paid for the pizza after eating half.

The speed at which she was rushed into testing told her that her meeting with Justin hadn't been by chance and that she owed him more than half a pizza next time they met. She'd asked after him a couple of times since she'd made it past the qualification exams—and the examiners' brutal interviews that had left her questioning her sanity, never mind her ability.

"Justin Roberts is presently deployed, ma'am," was the only response she'd ever gotten.

Now that she was through training—almost, had to be soon, didn't it?—Danielle realized that was probably less of an evasion and more likely to do with the brutal op tempo the Night Stalkers maintained. The SOAR 1st Battalion had just won the coveted Lt. General Ellis D. Parker awards for Outstanding Combat Aviation Battalion *and* Aviation Battalion of the Year. They'd been on deployment every single day of the last year, actually of the last decade-plus since 9/11.

The very first Special Forces boots on the ground in Afghanistan were delivered that October by the Night Stalkers and nothing had slacked off since. Justin might be in the 5th battalion D company, but they were just as heavily assigned as the 1st.

Part of their training had included tours in Afghanistan. But unlike any of their prior deployments, these were brief, intense, and then they'd be back in the States pushing to integrate their new skills.

SOAR needed her training to end and so did she.

Danielle was ready for the job, in her own, inestimable opinion. But she wasn't going to get there until the trainers signed off that she'd reached fully mission-qualified proficiency.

The Fort Campbell training course was never set up the same from one flight to the next, but it always had a time limit. The time would be short and they didn't tell you what it was. So she drove the Chinook for all it was worth like Regina Jaquess waterskiing her way to U.S. Ski Team Female Athlete of the Year.

The Night Stalkers were a damned secretive lot, and after two years of training, she understood why. With seven years flying for the 10th, she'd thought she was good.

She'd been repeatedly lauded as one of the top pilots at Fort Drum.

The Night Stalkers had offered an education in what it really meant to fly. In the two years of training, she'd flown more hours than in the seven years prior, despite two deployments to Iraq. And spent more time in the classroom than her life-to-date accumulated flight hours.

But she was ready now. It was *très viscérale*, right down in her bones she could feel it. The Chinook was as much a part of her nervous system as breathing.

Too bad they didn't build men the way they built the big Chinooks—especially the MH-47G which were built specifically to SOAR's requirements. The aircraft were steady, trustworthy, and the most immensely power-ful helicopters deployed in the U.S. Army—what more could a girl ask for? But finding a superhero man to go with her superhero helicopter was just a fantasy for a lonely teenage girl.

She dove down into a canyon and slid to

a hover mere inches over the reservoir inside the thirty-second window laid out on the flight plan.

Danielle resisted a sigh. She was ready for something to happen and to happen soon.

# # #

Pete's Chinook and his two escort Black Hawks crossed into the mountainous province of Sikkim, India ten feet over the glaciers and still moving fast. It was an hour before dawn, they'd made it out of China while it was still dark.

"Twenty minutes of fuel remaining," Nicolai said it like a personal challenge when they hit the border.

"Thanks, I never would have noticed."

It had been a nail-biting tradeoff: the more fuel he burned, the more easily he climbed due to the lighter load. The more he climbed, the faster he burned what little fuel remained.

Safe in Indian airspace he climbed hard as Nicolai counted down the minutes remaining, burning fuel even faster than he had been while crossing the mountains of southern Tibet. They caught up with the U.S. Air Force

HC-130P Combat King refueling tanker with only ten minutes of fuel left.

"Ram that bitch," Nicolai called out.

Pete extended the refueling probe which reached only a few feet beyond the forward edge of the rotor blade and drove at the basket trailing behind the tanker on its long hose.

He nailed it on the first try despite the fluky winds. Striking the valve in the basket with over four hundred pounds of pressure, a clamp snapped over the refueling probe and Jet A fuel shot into his tanks.

His helo had the least fuel due to having the most men aboard, so he was first in line. His Number Two picked up the second refueling basket trailing off the other wing of the Combat King. Thirty seconds and three hundred gallons later and he was breathing much more easily.

"Ah," Nicolai sighed. "It is better than the sex," his thick Russian accent only ever surfaced in this moment or in a bar while picking up women.

"Hey, Nicolai," Nicky the Greek called over the intercom from his crew chief position seated behind Pete. "Do you make love in Russian?"

A question Pete had always been careful to avoid.

"For you, I make special exception." That got a laugh over the system.

Which explained why Pete always kept his mouth shut at this moment.

"The ladies, Nicolai? What about the ladies?" Alfie the portside gunner asked.

"Ah," he sighed happily as he signaled that the other choppers had finished their refueling and formed up to either side, "the ladies love the Russian. They don't need to know I grew up in Maryland and I learn my great-great-grandfather's native tongue at the University called Virginia."

He sounded so pleased that Pete wished he'd done the same rather than study Japanese and Mandarin.

Another two hours of—thank god—straight-and-level flight at altitude through the breaking dawn and they landed on the aircraft carrier awaiting them in the Bay of Bengal. India had agreed to turn a blind eye as long as the Americans never actually touched their soil.

Once standing on the deck—and the worst

of the kinks had been worked out—he pulled his team together: six pilots and seven crew chiefs.

"Honor to serve!" He saluted them sharply.

"Hell yeah!" They shouted in response and saluted in turn. It was their version of spiking the football in the end zone.

A petty officer in a bright green vest appeared at his elbow, "Follow me please, sir." He pointed toward the Navy-gray command structure that towered above the carrier's deck.

The Commodore of the entire carrier group was waiting for him just outside the entrance. Not a good idea to keep a One-Star waiting, so he waved at the team.

"See you in the mess for dinner," he shouted to the crew over the noise of an F-18 Hornet fighter jet trapping on the #2 wire. After two days of surviving on MREs while squatting on the Tibetan tundra, he was ready for a steak, a burger, a mountain of pasta, whatever. Or maybe all three.

The green escorted him across the hazards of the busy flight deck. Pete had kept his helmet on to buffer the noise, but even at that he winced as another Hornet fired up and was flung aloft by the catapult.

"Orders, Major Napier," the Commodore handed him a folded sheet the moment he arrived. "Hate to lose you."

The Commodore saluted, which Pete automatically returned before looking down at the sheet of paper in his hands. The man was gone before the import of Pete's orders slammed in.

A different green-clad deckhand showed up with Pete's duffle bag and began guiding him toward a loading C-2 Greyhound twin-prop airplane. It was parked number two for the launch catapult, close behind the raised jet-blast deflector.

His crew, being led across in the opposite direction to return to the berthing decks below, looked at him aghast.

"Stateside," was all he managed to gasp out as they passed.

A stream of foul cursing followed him from behind. Their crew was tight. Why the hell was Command breaking it up?

And what in the name of fuck-all had he done to deserve this?

He glanced at the orders again as he stumbled up the Greyhound's rear ramp and crash landed into a seat.

Training rookies?

It was worse than a demotion.

This was punishment.

This and other titles are available at fine retailers everywhere.

Other works by M.L. Buchman

<u>The Night Stalkers</u>

MAIN FLIGHT

The Night Is Mine
I Own the Dawn
Wait Until Dark
Take Over at Midnight
Light Up the Night
Bring On the Dusk
By Break of Day

WHITE HOUSE HOLIDAY

Daniel's Christmas
Frank's Independence Day
Peter's Christmas
Zachary's Christmas
Roy's Independence Day

AND THE NAVY

Christmas at Steel Beach
Christmas at Peleliu Cove

5E

Target of the Heart
Target Lock on Love

<u>Firehawks</u>

MAIN FLIGHT

Pure Heat
Full Blaze
Hot Point
Flash of Fire

SMOKEJUMPERS

Wildfire at Dawn
Wildfire at Larch Creek
Wildfire on the Skagit

<u>Delta Force</u>
Target Engaged
Heart Strike

<u>Angelo's Hearth</u>
Where Dreams are Born
Where Dreams Reside
Maria's Christmas Table
Where Dreams Unfold
Where Dreams Are Written

<u>Eagle Cove</u>
Return to Eagle Cove
Recipe for Eagle Cove
Longing for Eagle Cove
Keepsake for Eagle Cove

<u>Deities Anonymous</u>
Cookbook from Hell: Reheated
Saviors 101

<u>Dead Chef Thrillers</u>
Swap Out!
One Chef!
Two Chef!

<u>SF/F Titles</u>
Nara
Monk's Maze
The Me and Elsie Chronicles

Newsletter signup at:
www.mlbuchman.com